Winter Comes
to Sheepfold Farm

a story by

Susan Williams

LONDON
VICTOR GOLLANCZ LTD
1984

For Lucy, Helen and Zoë

First published in Great Britain 1984
by Victor Gollancz Ltd,
14 Henrietta Street, London WC2E 8QJ

© 1984 Susan Williams

British Library Cataloguing in Publication Data
Williams, Susan, *1946–*
   Winter comes to Sheepfold Farm.
   I. Title
   823'.914[J]   PZ7

ISBN 0-575-03487-4

Photoset in Great Britain by
Rowland Phototypesetting Ltd, Bury St Edmunds, Suffolk
and printed by St Edmundsbury Press,
Bury St Edmunds, Suffolk

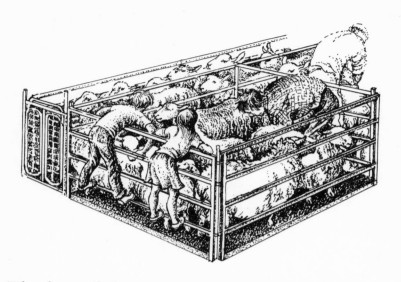

The last of the summer's corn crops had been gathered in. All over Chalkbourne Downs hedgerows were laden with ripening blackberries, elderberries and sloes.

Up at Field Barn, Polly and Tim were hanging over a gate, watching their father, Jack Evans, the shepherd at Sheepfold Farm, and Walt Roberts, the tractor driver, as they sorted out and prepared Jack's flock for the new breeding season.

September marked the beginning of the sheep year. Jack and Walt knew that the success of next spring's lambing mainly depended on the ewes and rams being in good condition at tupping time in the autumn. Tupping was the word shepherds used to describe sheep mating and they often called their rams tups.

Walt and Jack sweated in the warm sun, turning up every ewe to examine her teeth, udder and feet. Ewes with udder trouble were not kept for further breeding, and were sold for slaughter.

Broken mouth ewes, who were beginning to lose their teeth, would not do well next lambing in such a large flock. They, too, would be sold at the autumn fairs often to dairy farmers and smallholders wanting just a few sheep.

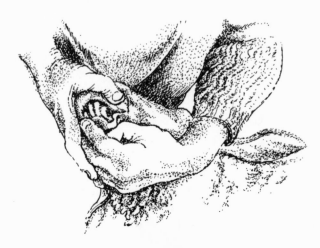

Walt and Jack cut away any overgrown or
diseased parts of the ewes' hooves with clippers
and then ran them through a footbath of
disinfectant.

On the way home for tea, Jack, Walt, Polly and Tim stopped to feed the fifty rams of the Sheepfold Farm flock. At the beginning of August, Jack had sorted through the rams, marking any that were to be sold with the culled ewes in September. Since then, he had been feeding extra barley and oats to the others so that they would be fit and active for mating with the ewes.

The feeding plan that Jack followed for his ewes was slightly different. Once the last of the lambs had been weaned he kept the ewes on short grazing for the rest of the summer, letting the over-fat ones scavenge on the sparse stubble fields. Then, about three weeks before tupping, he put all the ewes on to good grass and allowed them to eat well. This was called flushing.

"Why do sheep always lamb in the Spring?" asked Polly, as they watched the rams jostling for places at the feed troughs. She had never really thought about it before, but knew that horses, cows and pigs gave birth to their young at any time of year.

"It all starts with the shortening daylight hours after midsummer," explained Jack. "These act as a trigger and bring ewes of most breeds into season from August to the middle of December. The ewes can only be mated with the rams when they are in season, and it takes five months for the lambs to grow inside them from the time that they are conceived. So a ewe that is tupped in October will give birth to lambs in February or March."

A few days later, Polly and Tim were walking slowly across an old sheep pasture, searching for pink-gilled mushrooms that were beginning to grow in the fields.

Dark plumes of smoke and tongues of flame rose into the clear sky from burning stubble fields around. It was the end of harvest and most farmers were burning their unwanted straw and stubble. The fire cleaned and fertilised the soil, before the next crop was planted.

The children had half filled their baskets with mushrooms, when they reached a track running along the boundary of Sheepfold Farm.

The stubble fires were burning fiercely in a neighbouring farmer's field and both children hesitated as sudden gusts of wind blew smoke and flames in front of them, scorching trees and hedges.

They looked at some of Jack's over-fat ewes grazing peacefully across the track from the burning fields. Suddenly a wisp of loose burning straw was caught up into a whirlwind of hot air, carried a few yards and then dropped down on to the unburned stubble of the Sheepfold Farm field.

In a minute, a ripple of tiny flames sprang up.

There was no time to be lost. Polly and Tim knew how fast fire spread in dry straw; already it was too late to stamp it out.

"Quick Polly! We must get the sheep out of here! Go and open the gate in the far corner," shouted Tim. Luckily, the stubble was surrounded by grass fields which would not catch fire.

By now the flock had scented danger and were beginning to run in a blind panic. Tim tried vainly to gather them. If only he had one of his father's dogs, Floss, Tib or Patch. His eyes began to stream but he could just make out the open gateway and Polly running back around the sheep. Through the clouds of smoke, he glimpsed a lithe black and white shape streaking across the field.

"FLOSS! 'Way to me!" he yelled above the crackling roar of the flames. But the dog did not respond to the usual commands and began to make odd darting movements into the sheep, scattering them, instead of circling the flock. In desperation, Tim picked a blade of grass and, cupping his hands, whistled loudly on it.

The dog paused and then ran swiftly round the flock towards the sound. It was just enough to get the sheep moving in the direction of the gateway. Soon they were pouring into the grass field, flanked on either side by Polly, Tim and the dog—minutes before the fire caught them up.

The children ran a little way into the cool moist grass and flung themselves down.

When they looked up, the fire was nearly out, leaving a blackened smouldering field.

There was no sign of the dog anywhere.

"That's Higgins not ploughing a wide enough strip round his stubble. He always was careless," said Jack angrily, when Polly and Tim found him in the farmyard. "I'd better get up there double quick and make sure the fire is really out."

"It couldn't have been Floss or any of the dogs. They were shut up in their kennels here at home," said Betty, their mother, when she heard about the rescue of the sheep. But no one could shed any light on where the mystery dog came from.

Next day was the start of the autumn term. Polly and Tim set off for school, feeling hot and itchy in their new winter uniforms, gloomily thinking of the freedom and excitement of the summer holidays that were now over.

However, they were slightly cheered by the thought of a day at Chalkhill Bishop Great Fair the following week. Jack would be selling his culled sheep and buying in some new tups and breeding ewes for the flock, and Polly, Tim and Betty were going with him.

All over the country, in preparation for the autumn fairs, ram breeders were busy washing and clipping their rams' fleeces. It was skilful work, intended to emphasise the rams' deep chests and long, broad backs. Walt called it scornfully "an optical delusion".

On the morning of the Chalkhill Bishop Fair the well-groomed rams arrived in a variety of vehicles—some even in the back seats of cars.

Jack unloaded his ewes and rams from a lorry and, after driving them to their pens, he met up with his boss, Mr Fairweather. They went round the pens of rams and ewes, carefully noting down in their sale catalogues the ones they were interested in buying.

Polly, Tim and Betty enjoyed looking round

at the more unusual breeds of rams, which had enthusiastic owners hovering over them.

Polly thought the long crinkly fleece of a Wensleydale ram was beautiful, and wished Mr Fairweather would buy him for the Sheepfold Farm flock.

Dorset and Hampshire Down, and Suffolk rams were the most popular breeds in the area. Ewes that were mated with these rams gave birth to sturdy, fast-growing lambs.

The Hampshire and Dorset Down were stocky sheep, with broad, well fleshed rumps and brown ears and faces, framed by clumps of wool on their cheeks and foreheads.

The Suffolk was renowned for its long back, and fine glossy black head and legs.

Polly and Tim watched nervous breeders tap their prize rams around a ring to show them off at their best to prospective buyers.

"They are handsome creatures—no doubt about that," said Betty to Jack, gasping at the high prices some of the rams were fetching.

There was a bit of fighting when the rams bought at the fair were introduced to those already at the farm. Jack penned them up together for a few days to allow them to make friends. Walt made hay collars for the new rams to encourage the others to nuzzle them and so become used to their smell.

Some new ewe lambs arrived by lorry from the North as replacements for ewes sold at the fair, and Jack and Walt were kept busy all the following week, preparing them for tupping.

They were vaccinated to prevent them bringing any serious diseases to the flock and to give immunity to the lambs they would have in the future.

Then Jack round-tailed the ewe lambs by
shearing the wool away from their tails and
hindquarters. This made it easier for the rams to
mate with them properly.

Finally they were "drenched" with a special
medicine, which killed all the worms in their
digestive tracts, and flushed on fresh pasture.

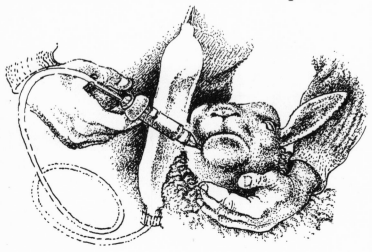

Next weekend, Polly and Tim gave Jack a hand cleaning the ram harnesses. At tupping time, each ram wore one of these so that, when he mated with a ewe, he left a coloured mark on

her rump from a special colour block called a crayon, fixed to the breast strap.

"Which colour will you use first, Dad?" asked Tim, as they worked away, saddle-soaping the stiff, mildewed leather.

"Blue for the early lambing flock, then red, then green for the April lambing lot," said Jack, tapping the old worn crayons from their holders with a hammer.

Jack and Walt had divided the fifteen hundred ewes at Sheepfold Farm into three flocks. The six hundred in best condition would go to the ram at the end of September. The rams would be put out wearing blue crayons in their harnesses and all those ewes marked blue at the end of two or three weeks made up the early flock, to begin lambing at the end of February.

Each flock of ewes would have been with teaser rams about two weeks before tupping began. Teasers were rams made infertile by an operation. Their presence stimulated the ewes to come into season so that when the fertile rams went out with them, they were tupped very quickly.

"What's so special about today?" said Polly as she and Tim scrambled for their schoolbags one morning towards the end of September. The sheep calendar hanging in the kitchen was marked with a big red circle around the twenty-seventh.

"Have you forgotten?" laughed Betty. "This is the day the rams go out with the early flock!"

Polly and Tim left the shepherd's cottage in good time for school and ran up the lane.

They could see Jack and Walt ahead of them, unloading rams from the Land Rover and trailer, which were parked by the gateway to a field called Toby's Bottom. Jack had split the ewes into two lots of three hundred and since one mature ram would tup up to forty or fifty ewes, he was putting ten rams in with each flock.

The rams lumbered down the ramp of the trailer. A group of ewes detached themselves from the rest of the flock and went forward to meet them.

"It looks as though the teasers have done their job," said Walt.

When the ewes were in season and ready to

mate, their smell attracted the rams. A ewe and a ram would become especially interested in each other and circle round, nuzzling and talking. The ewe would allow the ram to jump up and straddle her back with his forelegs, so that his chest was resting on her rump. In this position, he could successfully mate with her.

"The rams are working well—time to change the colour crayon and to put more rams out with the next lot of ewes," said Jack to Betty several weeks later, when he had counted five hundred blue-bottomed ewes. That was a big enough flock to fill the lambing site at Field Barn.

The kitchen of the shepherd's cottage was fragrant with the smells of fruit pies and bubbling saucepans of jam and chutney. Betty was preparing food for the harvest supper to be held in the village hall.

Everyone looked forward to this annual feast, and this year it turned out to be as much fun as

ever. The three Sheepfold Farm tractor drivers, Walt, Bob White and Bert Penny, got quite merry on the cider and there were lots of speeches and songs, and ragging between the arable workers, cowmen and shepherds.

Jack and the other shepherds compared prices they had obtained for their fat lambs and swopped stories about the lambing season and the summer's sheep rustling.

Brenda Roberts, Walt's niece who was shepherdess at Blagdon Farm, offered Jack some autumn "keep" for his ewes; two crops of stubble turnips that her own flock did not need.

The days grew shorter and a nip of autumn was in the air. Jack bought himself a new winter hat.

One weekend, Polly and Tim were collecting conkers from the big old horse chestnut tree in the farmyard, when the shepherd's van drew up with a jerk and Jack got out. Polly and Tim could tell he was in a rage and scurried after him, asking what the matter was.

"It's those ewes in Toby's Bottom—found 'em in a terrible state this morning, driven against the fence and as jittery as frightened cats," he told them later over a cup of coffee.

Betty stroked Beulah their grey cat, who was tightly curled up in her lap. "It couldn't be rustlers again, could it—have you counted the ewes?"

"No, a dog has had a go at them," said Jack. "There are several with torn fleeces and nips on their flanks. This'll cost us a few lambs."

The first weeks of a ewe's pregnancy were a risky time for the developing lamb embryos. The mother could easily lose her lambs if she was roughly handled or frightened.

Jack borrowed Mr Fairweather's gun and stayed down in Toby's Bottom a few nights, hoping to catch the culprit. Farmers were entitled to shoot dogs they caught worrying their livestock.

But whatever it was that had stirred up the sheep, did not return.

Towards the end of October, Jack had a phone call from Brenda Roberts to say that the stubble turnips were ready.

Jack wanted to keep his crops of kale and swedes in reserve for as long as possible. But he would soon have to think about giving the ewes extra food, because the late autumn grass no longer contained enough nourishment for them and their developing lambs. So he was glad of Brenda's offer.

"We'll walk the early flock along the old ox drove tomorrow," he said to Walt. "Since it's half term, maybe Polly, Tim and Betty will help."

Early in the morning, the dogs gathered the blue flock and twelve rams from a field near the

drove and they set off at a gentle pace towards
Blagdon Farm.

"Steady there!" roared Jack at the dogs every
now and then, worried that they were driving
the pregnant ewes too hard.

Among the blue flock was Lop Ear, Polly and
Tim's favourite ewe who had been stolen by
rustlers in the summer. The children were sorry
that Lop Ear had not yet been marked by a ram.
Any ewe who was not pregnant by the end of
tupping time was called a barrener and usually
sent to market in the Spring, unless she was a
young one.

"This puts me in mind of when I was a boy," said Walt as they settled down to have a snack half way between Sheepfold Farm and Blagdon.

The sheep grazed at the edges of the drove under the watchful eyes of the dogs.

"Did you help with the sheep in those days?" asked Betty.

"My old dad was shepherd for the Watsons—just over the ridge there—and we used to drive the sheep to Chalkhill Bishop Fairs along this drove. Folks have used it for hundreds of years to drive cattle and sheep to market. It used to be kept trimmed right back. Now look how over-grown it is."

Polly wondered how shepherds going to the fair stopped their different flocks mixing up.

"Well, in them days we had the Old English sheepdogs—there weren't the collies about then, y'know," explained Walt, "and although they was such great hairy things, they could work. We relied on them to keep the flocks apart."

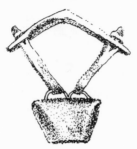

They came down off the drove at Blagdon and
Brenda directed them to one of her spare fields of
stubble turnips.

The sheep would be put on to a narrow strip
(or fold) of turnips and allowed to eat from
morning until nightfall. Then Brenda's dog, Fly,
would bring them back on to an adjoining grass
field for the night.

When they had completely eaten the turnips in
the netted piece, Brenda would take up the divid-
ing fence and let them into a fresh fold. So they
would move across the whole field, grazing each
piece thoroughly until the whole crop was eaten
off.

Jack reckoned the two fields would last about
eight weeks. "We'll bring 'em back just before
Christmas," he said.

For the rest of the half term holiday, Polly and Tim got up early each day, to check round the sheep with Jack. On Friday morning, they stopped at Pug's Hole, where three hundred of the red flock were grazing, and peered through the thick autumnal mist. There was no sign of the ewes or the rams. Polly picked up handfuls of wool, scattered over the frosty grass.

"As I expected," said Jack grimly, when they found a ewe badly tangled in a wire fence and the rest of the flock huddled together in a nervous heap. "Sheep worriers again."

"We must get to the bottom of this—I'll stay up there tonight with my gun," said Mr Fairweather, when Jack told him what had happened.

That evening was Hallowe'en and Polly and Tim planned to go tricking or treating round the village with their friends.

Someone had given them two big pumpkins and they scooped out the pulp and cut grinning faces in the shells.

As soon as darkness fell, Rosie and George Hawkins and a gang of others came knocking at the shepherd's cottage door. Polly and Tim were just fixing night lights into the pumpkin lanterns.

Floss, Tib and Patch growled from their kennels in the yard at the weird crew clustered round the doorstep and at the witch and ghost who swept out to join them.

"Back by eight-thirty, mind!" Betty shouted after the golden globes of light bobbing down the lane.

They rapped on window panes and made
spooky noises through letterboxes. Most people
chose to give a treat, such as an orange or an
apple and a mug of something hot, rather than
risk being booby trapped.

Their last stop on the way home was at a
newly renovated cottage called *The Nook*.

"Waah!" wailed Rosie Hawkins through the
letterbox and the door was opened cautiously. A
woman with a plump, kind face peered out at
them. When she saw their homemade disguises
and the pumpkin lanterns, she gave them an
uncertain smile.

"You gave us a scare with that horrible racket —we'd got to expect fireworks and the like being pushed through our door in the town. You'd better come in—what is it you're after?"

They trooped through the warm lighted hall into a comfortable, chintzy living room where the woman's husband and a collie were watching sheepdog trials on television. The dog followed the flickering pictures of sheep on the screen and whined excitedly, ears erect, after every command and whistle.

The programme was just ending and the woman's husband reluctantly turned the television off.

They chatted about the village and surrounding farms and ate Mrs Bailey's tasty shortbread.

Mr and Mrs Bailey were newcomers to Chalk-bourne. They told the children how they had moved from the town when they had retired.

"Thought it would be lovely, but we're finding it hard to make friends," sighed Mrs Bailey.

"That's why we got Jess," said Mr Bailey, toeing the silky flank at his feet. "We've always loved border collies since we've seen them working on that telly programme—wonderful dogs."

"My Dad says collies kept as pets are a proper nuisance," said Rosie Hawkins.

"Now and then she strays off when we let her out at night," went on Mrs Bailey, not noticing Rosie's disapproval. "Yesterday evening she didn't come back till the small hours."

Tim caught Polly's eye. Could it be Jess who was worrying the Sheepfold Farm sheep?

Polly shivered and thought of Mr Fair-weather, lying in wait up at Pug's Hole with his gun. Jess lay stretched out on the hearthrug, looking as though butter wouldn't melt in her mouth.

Much later than half past eight, Polly and Tim hurried back along the lane to Sheepfold Farm. As they rounded the last bend, a dark shape overtook them on the other side of the hedge.

Both children started nervously. They remembered a story told by Walt of a shepherd and his dog who had frozen to death in a snow-storm in Pug's Hole many years ago. But somehow that shape was familiar . . .

"Jess!" cried Polly in dismay. "Come on Tim, we've got to stop Mr Fairweather shooting her!"

They found Mr Fairweather hiding in a clump of gorse overlooking the sheep who were camped in hollows about the field.

Polly and Tim barely had time to tell him about Jess, before she appeared out of the hedge line. In a trice she was causing panic among the sleeping sheep. Leaping and snapping, she ran this way and that, until finally she singled out one ewe and chased her relentlessly up and down the field.

"Let us try to call her, we know the owners, they'll be terribly upset if you shoot her," pleaded Polly.

"I'll give you one chance to call her off. Be quick—before she pulls the ewe down," said Mr Fairweather, his hand on his gun.

"Jessie! Heel!" called Tim urgently.

But the dog took no notice.

Tim picked a blade of grass and whistled with all his might.

Jess stopped dead in her tracks. Polly and Tim ran down the field calling her all the time. She began to trot towards them, wagging her tail.

Mr and Mrs Bailey were very relieved to have Jess back and shocked to hear about the sheep worrying. By now, Polly and Tim were sure she was the mysterious dog who had helped push the ewes out of the burning field. They described the fierce stubble fire and how Jess had not responded to Tim's commands until he whistled on a blade of grass.

"She might have been a good working dog if she'd been trained as a pup," said Mr Fairweather gruffly, "but if I ever catch her worrying my sheep again—I won't give her a second chance."

The second half of the autumn term was tidying up time on the farm. Most of the stubble fields had been ploughed up and the winter corn planted. The last fields to be ploughed would be left unsewn until March when the spring corn would be put in.

Jack and Walt repaired broken sheep-fences and dipped all the wattle hurdles in creosote (a preservative) ready for next lambing.

Walt, Bert and Bob trimmed back hedgerows, cut down dead trees and lit huge brushwood

bonfires in the fields. On November the fifth,
Jack changed the colour in the rams' harnesses
from red to green and put more rams out with
the last five hundred ewes.

Polly, Tim and Rosie Hawkins and her gang often called in to see Mr and Mrs Bailey in the dark autumn days following Hallowe'en.

Polly and Tim took Jess out for extra walks, taking care to have her on a lead when near cattle and sheep. They practised getting the Baileys' chickens in at night with her. She was quick to learn and becoming very obedient.

The winter days grew shorter and soon it was December.

Mrs White stocked the village shop with Christmas goodies and hung the window with tinsel and paper chains.

Chalkbourne school hummed with excitement and the children began to rehearse their Christmas nativity play. Polly and Tim were to be two of the three shepherds, but they were horrified at the fluffy toy lamb Miss Jenkins wanted them to carry.

"It doesn't look anything like a real lamb," grumbled Polly, "if only we had some on the farm . . ."

"Brenda's phoned to say the blues have nearly finished the stubble turnips at Blagdon," said Betty to Jack, one Friday afternoon near the end of term.

"We'll walk them back on Sunday—they were looking pretty fit when I saw them last week," said Jack.

On Sunday afternoon, Walt dropped the Evans family off at Blagdon Farm and they all walked up to the stubble turnips where they met Brenda. They thanked her for looking after the Sheepfold Farm sheep and Jack whistled to his dogs to bring the flock out of the field.

"Happy Christmas!" shouted Polly and Tim, looking back and waving as they walked behind the sheep, along a track up to the drove.

Holly trees bright with scarlet berries, and dark yews, leaned over the old green road. Polly and Tim broke off boughs to take home for Christmas decorations.

They were about three quarters of the way back to Sheepfold Farm, and the light was fading fast, when Polly and Tim noticed Lop Ear dropping behind the rest of the flock. Finally she refused to be driven any further and turned on the dogs, butting them angrily.

"What's the matter with her Mum, is she ill?" Polly asked Betty.

Betty walked over to where Lop Ear stood, with sides heaving and head down.

"Good heavens! She's lambing!" she said after a few minutes.

They were all worried at first that the lambs would be tiny premature things. But Lop Ear gave birth to a fine healthy pair of twins, very white with little horn stubs showing on their heads.

Jack looked puzzled. "Full term lambs all right—where did you get 'em from my girl? No Dorset Down or Suffolk ram fathered these!" he said.

"She must have been tupped in July," said Betty "no wonder our rams didn't mark her."

"Maybe she got with a ram when the rustlers had her—a Dorset Horn by the looks of those lambs," said Jack.

"We should have noticed that she was bagged up," said Betty. About two or three weeks before lambing, a pregnant ewe's udder would become much larger as it filled with milk.

It was nightfall by the time the early lambing flock reached Sheepfold Farm.

Bringing up the rear, came Polly and Tim, each carrying a newborn lamb, and closely followed by Lop Ear.

Polly and Tim came home from school on
Monday, cross and tired after the final dress
rehearsal in the village church.

Polly had persuaded Miss Jenkins to let them
bring one of Lop Ear's beautiful lambs as the
shepherds' gift to Jesus. But the lamb bawled
loudly, drowning the infants' carol, while Polly,
Tim and Dan Stewart processed up the aisle
to the chancel steps.

Then it wriggled free from Tim's arms as they
were kneeling at the manger and ran off, nuzzling everybody's legs in search of milk.

"The thing to do," said Jack when he heard
about these disasters, "is to tuck a bottle of Lop
Ear's milk into your shepherd's pouch and give
the lamb a good feed whenever it gets restless."

Tuesday was the night of the nativity play and
after school Polly and Tim ran down the lane to
the village to ask Mr and Mrs Bailey to come.

The sky was studded with brilliant stars and
little decorated Christmas trees winked and glit-
tered in the cottage windows of Chalkbourne.

Before going indoors, Polly and Tim went to see Lop Ear and her lambs, snug in a wattle hurdle pen with a roof which Jack had made for her in the garden.

Lop Ear stood quietly while Tim squeezed some milk from her warm, full udder, into a bottle.

Polly picked up her smaller lamb. "It's all right girl, we'll bring him back soon," she said.

All Chalkbourne school assembled in the
church vestry, where some volunteer mums
helped them to dress in their costumes. The
infants peeped through the vestry curtains to
wave at the audience gathering in the nave.

Garlands of holly and ivy tumbled from every pillar and window-ledge; candles shimmered in the choir stalls. Polly and Tim thought they had never seen the church look so beautiful.

Gradually a hush fell on the chattering audience as all but a few lights were turned out and the low sweet tones of "Once in Royal David's City" filled the old stone building.

The juniors sang like angels and the infants remembered nearly all their words.

The three kings strode up the aisle in their royal robes, drawing murmurs of admiration from the audience.

The shepherds walked slowly and humbly to the manger with Polly playing "Oh Leave Your Sheep" on her recorder, while Tim carried Lop Ear's lamb, nestling drowsily in his arms.

Jack and Betty thought about their flocks sleeping on the Downs and of the busy lambing season to come.

"We wish you a Merry Christmas,
And a Happy New Year . . ."
sang Mary, Joseph, angels, kings, shepherds and all the children of Chalkbourne school, grinning broadly at the prospect of the glorious holidays ahead.

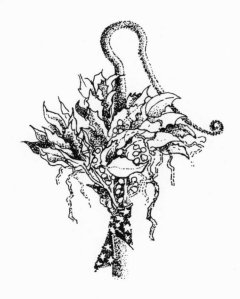